THE COLOR KITTENS

BY MARGARET WISE BROWN

ILLUSTRATED BY ALICE AND MARTIN PROVENSEN

GOLDEN PRESS
Western Publishing Company, Inc.
Racine, Wisconsin

Fifteenth Printing, 1980

Once there were two color kittens with green eyes, Brush and Hush. They liked to mix and make colors by splashing one color into another. They had buckets and buckets

and buckets and buckets of color to splash around with. Out of these colors they would make all the colors in the world.

The buckets had the colors written on them, but of course the kittens couldn't read. They had to tell by the colors. "It is very easy," said Brush.

"Red is red. Blue is blue," said Hush.

But they had no green. "No green paint!" said Brush and Hush. And they wanted green paint, of course, because nearly every place they liked to go was green.

Green as cats' eyes
Green as grass
By streams of water
Green as glass.

So they tried to make some green paint.

Brush mixed red paint and white paint together—and what did that make? It didn't make green.

But it made pink.

Pink as pigs

Pink as toes

Pink as a rose
Or a baby's nose.

Then Hush mixed yellow and red together, and it made orange.

Orange as an orange tree

Orange as a bumblebee

Orange as the setting sun
Sinking slowly in the sea.

The kittens were delighted, but it didn't make green.

Then they mixed red and blue together—and what did that make? It didn't make green. It made a deep dark purple.

Purple as violets

Purple as plums

Purple as shadows
On late afternoons.

Still no green! And then . . .

O wonderful kittens! O Brush! O Hush!

At last, almost by accident, the kittens poured a bucket of blue and a bucket of yellow together, and it came to pass that they made a green as green as grass.

Green as green leaves on a tree

Green as islands in the sea.

The little kittens were so happy with all the colors they had made that they began to paint everything around them. They painted . . .

Green leaves
and red berries
and purple flowers
and pink cherries
Red tables
and yellow chairs
Black trees
with golden pears.

Then the kittens got so excited they knocked their buckets upside down and all the colors ran together. Yellow, red, a little blue and a little black . . . and that made brown.

Brown as a tugboat

Brown as an old goat

Brown as a beaver

And in all that brown, the sun went down. It was evening and the colors began to disappear in the warm dark night.

The kittens fell asleep in the warm dark night with all their colors out of sight and as they slept they dreamed their dream—

A wonderful dream
Of a red rose tree
That turned all white
When you counted three

One . . . Two . . .

Three

Of a purple land
In a pale pink sea

Where apples fell
From a golden tree

And then a world of Easter eggs
That danced about on little short legs.

And they dreamed that
A green cat danced
With a little pink dog

Till they all disappeared in a soft gray fog.

And suddenly Brush woke up and Hush woke up. It was morning. They crawled out of bed into a big bright world. The sky was wild with sunshine.

The kittens were wild with purring and pouncing—

They got so pouncy they knocked over the buckets and all the colors ran out together.

There were all the colors in the world and the color kittens had made them.